What is a Key Word?

A *Key Word* is a common w[...]
sight. They are the building [...]
appear so often. School rea[...]
Words so whatever scheme [...]
books will support it, they wil[...]
learning and develop his/her reading confidence and fluency.

Although *Key Words* are so common they are not always easy to learn. Most children find it much harder to remember 'the' than 'apple'. One of the reasons for this is that mentally they can make a picture of an apple, but they cannot make a mental picture for 'the'. Your child will need lots of encouragement.

What is an Incidental Word?

Other words, which are not *Key Words*, are introduced in the stories. This has been done to develop the second of the reading skills, that is, 'context'. The idea is that your child should try to guess the word by a) looking at the picture, b) thinking of a word which would make sense in the context of the sentence and story, and c) looking at the first letter of the word and thinking of a word that makes sense and starts with the right sound. Your child does not need to remember incidental words.

Attempting to read unknown words is very important. It is essential that you give your child lots of praise for a sensible guess. Never criticise an attempt, however wild. If the guess is wrong, supply the correct word, while praising the attempt.

Create a Feeling of Success

Your child must feel a sense of achievement for everything he/she reads. No matter how simple you think it is, give masses of praise. Young children need to feel that things are easy for them. If your child finds reading difficult, proceed very gently; find something which is easy so that he/she can develop a sense of success. Then you can pile on the praise and he/she will want to do more. Above all, don't push at this early stage. Keep it light-hearted and fun.

How to Use This Book

1 Write down the Key Words and show them to your child.
   Discuss the shape of the word, how many letters, what letter
   each starts with, etc. Write the words on separate cards and
   see if your child can learn one or two before starting the
   book. Find a page where a particular word appears and ask
   your child to point to the word.

2 If your child is quite confident, he/she might be happy to
   read straightaway. Otherwise, read the story aloud to your
   child first, pointing to each word as you do so. Spend time
   talking about the pictures because a great deal of the story
   is told in the pictures.

3 Ask questions, such as, 'What do you think will happen
   next?' Or 'Why did she do that?'

4 When your child starts to read the book, be very patient and
   encouraging. Never let him/her struggle over a word.
   Tell him/her what the word is.

5 Once you have reached the end of the book, encourage
   your child to read it as often as possible. One reading is not
   enough to learn the Key Words.

6 Use any of the activities suggested on page 28.

7 The text is specially designed to be read by a child who only
   knows the Key Words taught in this reading series.
   For this reason, you should start with the books in Level One
   and progress in order.

8 Avoid pressure and stress at all costs. Reading is fun.

Key Words introduced in this book:

It   was   went   out   of
the   They   to   on   home

Incidental Words:
**night   Sam   asleep   Bouncy   gate   crossed   road
park   busy   slide   fun   climbing-frame
roundabout   felt   dizzy**

age 4-6

Key Words
readers
Silky and Bouncy

Written by Nicola Morgan MA
an experienced teacher with a diploma in literacy teaching
Illustrations by Tina Freeman

Give lots of praise for reading, and stick the gold star reward sticker at the bottom of each right-hand page.

Key Words are printed in the coloured band at the foot of the page for the parent's reference.

Series editor: Nina Filipek
Series designer: Paul Dronsfield
Copyright © 1999 Egmont World Limited.
All rights reserved.
Published in Great Britain in 1999 by
Egmont World Limited, Deanway Technology Centre,
Wilmslow Road, Handforth, Cheshire SK9 3FB.
Printed in Germany.
ISBN 0 7498 4097 8

It was night.

Sam was asleep.

It was

It was night.

Silky went out.

It was night.

Bouncy went out.

Bouncy went out of
the gate.

Silky went out of the gate.

of the

They crossed the road.

They

They went to the park.

It was busy.

They went on the slide.

It was fun.

They went on the climbing-frame.

It was fun.

They went on the roundabout.

It was fun.

Can you see Silky
and Bouncy?

Silky and Bouncy felt dizzy.

They went home.

home

Reading is not just identifying the words in a story. To be an effective reader, and to enjoy reading, your child needs to understand, appreciate and respond to a story in different ways.

Here are some useful activities for you to do with your child. The activities will help iron out any difficulties and will extend your child's enjoyment and appreciation of the story.

It is vital that all reading activities are fun, so do give plenty of praise; never push your child too much or work when he/she is tired, cross or hungry.

Reading skills: although using clues from the pictures is an important part of early reading, we also want to encourage your child to concentrate on the print. To help develop this skill, write each sentence on a strip of card and ask your child to find the same sentence in the book.

Writing: later, when your child writes stories, he/she will need to be able to describe things and select details. Here is a fun activity to develop this: you and your child sit on either side of a table, with something propped between you as a screen. Each person has the same objects behind the screen (e.g. apple, banana, spoon, ball, teddy, biscuit, orange, pen, crayon, string). One person chooses an object then describes it, without using its name; the other person has to guess what it is.

Story-telling: ask your child to imagine what his/her toys might get up to at night.

Art: make a shadow play. Cut out silhouette shapes of animals and stick them on drinking straws. In a dark room, you and your child can hold the silhouettes and make up a little story or play.

Link to other areas of the curriculum: environmental studies. Visit the library and show your child how to find out which animals are awake at night and which are asleep. Teach your child the special word 'nocturnal'.

5 Great GIFTS
to choose from

In many of the new Egmont World books you will find a special token. It is on the following page in this book. Start collecting the tokens to make massive savings on this exclusive range of products.

1

£5.99 RSP
only £3.99 (+p&p)
with 5 tokens
The stationery set, packed in a plastic carrying case, comes complete with many items, including a pencil case and set squares.

2

£5.99 RSP
only £3.99 (+p&p)
with 5 tokens
The teaching clock has special hands that move just like a real clock.

3

£3.99 RSP
only £1.99 (+p&p)
with 5 tokens
The pencil case has an integral calculator.

4 **5**

99p RSP **FREE with 2 tokens**
Choose either the alphabet or the times tables poster.

If you have any difficulty finding the other books in this series please contact Egmont World Ltd. on 01625 650011

SAVE UP TO **£2 OFF** *Exclusive Gifts*

ONE TOKEN

Simply decide which gift you would like and collect the correct number of tokens. The more you collect the more money you can save.

	one token	two tokens	three tokens	four tokens	five tokens	
1 stationery case	£5.99 ☐	£5.49 ☐	£4.99 ☐	£4.49 ☐	£3.99 ☐	
2 teaching clock	£5.99 ☐	£5.49 ☐	£4.99 ☐	£4.49 ☐	£3.99 ☐	**MAXIMUM 5 TOKENS**
3 calculator pencil case	£3.99 ☐	£3.49 ☐	£2.99 ☐	£2.49 ☐	£1.99 ☐	
4 alphabet poster	£0.49 ☐	FREE ☐				**MAXIMUM 2 TOKENS**
5 times tables poster	£0.49 ☐	FREE ☐				

Please tick the offer you require above. You may also use the tokens available in other Egmont World books.

Please complete the following details:

I enclose a cheque made payable to Egmont World Limited for £_____ (inc. p+p) Please send me the gift(s) I have indicated.

Name _____

Age _____

Address _____

_____

_____

Postcode _____

Title of this book purchased

_____

Where it was purchased

_____

Offer open to residents of UK, Channel Isles and Ireland only. Please allow 14 days for delivery. Egmont World Ltd. withholds the right to withdraw the offer. Offer subject to availability.

Please return this completed form together with your tokens and a cheque or p.o. to:

Activity Centre Offers, Egmont World Limited, PO Box 7, Manchester M19 2HD.

Special Token

Please tape a £1 coin below to cover part post and packing costs.

£1

PLEASE STICK TOKENS BELOW

Place first token here	save 50p	save 50p	save 50p	save 50p

Once you have collected the required number of tokens, stick them to the spaces provided here and complete the form above.